Shadows of the Past
The Damien Blackwell Chronicles

Lee Alexander

Lee Alexander

Shadow Pages Press — Virginia Beach, VA
ISBN: 979-8-9911360-0-6
Library of Congress Control Number: pending
Title: *Shadows of the Past: The Damien Blackwell Chronicles*
Author: Lee Alexander
Digital distribution | 2024
Paperback | 2024

This is a work of fiction. The characters, names, incidents, places, and dialogue are products of the author's imagination, and are not to be construed as real.

Published in the United States by New Book Authors Publishing

Dedication

Dedicated to my Dad, William Alexander (1936-2021),

Your presence remains strong in my life, and I still hear "ALRIGHT!" whenever good things happen.

To my family and friends,

For your unwavering encouragement and belief in my storytelling.

And to my friend and mentor, Chris M,

Thank you for your relentless support and candid critiques. Your honest feedback challenged me to rethink and refine my craft, and for that, I am profoundly grateful.

Chapter 1

In the shadowed fog-laden streets of Victorian London, England, where the gaslights flickered like the last breath of the dying, Damien prowled the night. Cloaked in darkness and laden with ancient relics, along with an undying resolve and the cold steel of his great grandfather's sword, he was a Demon Slayer for hire. The city was a labyrinth of secrets, sins, and darkness few knew. Whispers of his deeds were murmured in hushed tones. He was a lone warrior, as were his father, grandfather, and great-grandfather before him, battling the infernal creatures that preyed on and tormented the weak-minded. He stood as the last defense in a world teetering on the brink of darkness, his life dedicated to the relentless pursuit of dark beings that dare prey on the innocent and the damned alike.

The whispers of his name stirred the air like a cursed incarnation, sending shivers down the spines of both mortal and demon alike. Each step he took was a descent into the bowels of a city corrupted by unspeakable horrors, where the line between man and monster blurred beneath the moon's pallid gaze. Here, in the underbelly of 1835 London, amidst the forsaken and forgotten, Damien confronted abominations that defied the average person's knowledge of nature itself. Creatures born from the darkest depths of the seven layers of hell, their grotesque forms shrouded by the mist that rises from the Thames and the dark air created by homes burning soft coal for warmth.

As Damien made his way through the streets towards the home of his next client, he was lost in deep consideration of what his life meant. Was he a holy man, a good man, or just another darkness that craves the night? He knew his lineage and birthright made his life worth less to most, but his skills made him invaluable to several. Does skill outweigh heritage and morality? Did his worth to others make his self-worth valuable to him? These were the demons that plagued his mind and ones he could not vanquish into the seven layers of Hell. These demons he must live with until either he can come to terms with them, atone for them, or accept them as his true self and reality. Until he can do one of these, his mind will be haunted by the demons that rule him.

As Damien approaches his destination, a two-story house built out of river stones, a thatched roof, and a wooden door. It is no different to all the other homes in this part of London. Not a hovel and not a mansion, but a simple home for a family of meager financial means. Damien quickly memorized the house's layout in case he needed a quick exit, or a fast pursuit ensued. As he approached the home, the front door swung open and closed behind him. The new Vicar, Vicar Thomas, was a man in his mid-twenties, about 183 centimeters tall, with brown hair and brown eyes. He was quite handsome in his black suit and cravat. He quickly approached Damien, carrying his Bible and Rosary, looking a little shaken with a look of terror on his face.

Vicar Thomas urgently approached Damien and asked, "You're the demon hunter, I presume?"

"I am Damien, the one your Cardinal sent for," responded Damien.

The Vicar gave a half smile and said, "Cardinal Maximus said you would be here before midnight."

"Have the midnight bells tolled, and I did not hear them?" replied Damien.

The Vicar looked him over and snorted, "I guess they have not. I am just a person who is very particular about schedules and quite nervous since this is all new to me."

Damien said, "It's alright now, and I have it from here. All I need you to do is lock the door behind me, do not come in, and do not unlock it for any reason."

At this, Damien opened the door and walked into the house. As he stepped into the house, the

Vicar closed the door behind him and locked it from the outside as he was instructed to do. Once inside, Damien surveyed the room the best he could with the small single candle lit on the table in the middle of the room. Shadows danced on the walls from the dim light, which made each item in the room a possible hiding place. Damien stepped further in and placed his satchel on the table, then neatly hung his cloak on the hooks on the wall near the door. He strolled around as if he was there for a visit and no other purpose.

With a calm and cautious demeanor, Damien stepped back to the table and opened his satchel. He reached in and removed some items one at a time. The first item he pulled was a candle that stood about 15 centimeters tall and 6 centimeters around. It was made of white wax with silver shavings in the wax, along with a red seal in the center of it and some runes carved into it. This was a Lumiara Decaflame, The Deca for short, a candle that was created by his great-great-grandfather, and the making of them passed down over the generations. The candle produced a light that demons could not resist coming to. It is not known if it is the light, the silver, the heat it produces, or something else. He removed the small candle from the holder on the table and turned it sideways to put some hot wax on the holder. Then, he pressed The Deca into the hot wax so that it stood up and lit it with the other candle and snuffed the small candle out. The Deca began to shine with the brightness of ten of the finest candles. The light began to bathe the room in its warm glow and created a cascade of shadows so small that no being could be hiding in them.

With the grand illumination of The Deca, Damien had a much better view of everything in the room, and he looked about, taking in the entirety of the room's content. There was the table he was standing at with four wooden chairs around it. Each chair had a small cushion on the seat to ease the feeling of hardwood against a person's buttocks. There was a small floral couch and a matching armchair in front of a cold fireplace, along with a painting of the King and an oil lamp on either side of the chimney on the wall. The one window in the room had the shutters drawn on the outside, and a curtain drawn closed. Next to the window was a painting of a country landscape that did not look familiar to Damien. In the corner of the room, just next to the fireplace, was a ladder leading up to the second floor of the home. The opening to the second floor was a very dark square hole in the ceiling. The darkness gave off no indication of what was up there, but Damien assumed there were sleeping quarters since no other accommodations could be seen.

With the candle burning bright, Damien pulled out the chair closest to the wall behind him and took a seat. He began to remove the rest of the items from his satchel and laid them out very neatly. Each item he removed was a religious item from the three major religions of the world. From the Catholic faith, he has a small wooden cross the size of a small dagger, a small vial of holy water from Saint Paul's Cathedral, another vial with an atomizer attached to it that looks to be empty, and a very well-worn Bible. From the Jewish faith, he has a pendant of the Star of David and a handwritten copy of the Tanakh. Lastly, from the Islamic faith, there was a copy of the Quran and a pendant in the shape of a crescent moon and a star. A leader of the corresponding faith blessed each item.

Part of Damien's year was visiting with each of the faith leaders and receiving a blessing on the items he carried and upon him. Each of the faith leaders put their trust and unconditional blessings upon him so that Damien may ensure the safety of all their followers. Damien also knew that this, in a way, made him a slave to these faiths, even though he was paid well for what he did. Damien's travels took him across the ocean to Vatican City for an audience with the Pope, where he received the Catholic blessing from the highest of the holy men in the church. Once he returned to London, he visited the Chief Rabbi to receive his Jewish blessing, and then he visited the Imam in the Islamic temple to be blessed by him. These blessings each year kept Damien and his artifacts at the peak of their holy affiliations and repulsive to those who sought to do harm to the faithful.

As Damien looked around the room, he did not notice any movement and was considering going up the ladder to the second floor. He wondered if there was anyone up there since he failed to ask the Vicar if anyone was still in the house. He continued to survey the room and take a mental inventory of everything he could see. All the while, Damien continued to look for anything out of the ordinary or something that may just not look to belong in the house. As his eyes crossed the ladder, there was a bit of movement in the shadow it cast into a dark corner. The shadow of the ladder appeared to be moving like water flowing down a waterfall. Damien continued to look around and pretend that he did not see the movement but kept his eyes looking for where the movement was going. From what he could ascertain, it was flowing down the ladder, across the floor, and under the table towards where Damien was seated. He began to run scenarios through his mind, wondering if the demon was going to take a seat, if it would come up to The Deca, or if it would try to grab Damien and pull him under the table.

Damien moved one hand to the hilt of his sword, and his other hand slowly passed over the artifacts on the table. As his hand passed over the artifacts, the Christian cross radiated warmth from it, and he took hold of the cross. This was telling him that whatever was coming was not a friend of Christians. Once Damien had the cross tightly in his grasp, he smiled and tensed his muscles, readying himself for what may come. As he was preparing, Damien could feel movement under the table and knew that whatever was flowing across the floor had begun to take a physical form more than the mist it was before.

Damien spoke out to the room, "Why not join me at the table and let me send you back to your home."

A dark shadow of a horned beast appeared across the table from Damien and grumbled, "What makes you think you have any power over me?"

"You have no host, so having power over you is an easy task," replied Damien.

The demon replied, "I am still more powerful than you and your puny trinkets."

Damien chuckled, smiled, and said, "The only ones with power over me are the spiritual leaders that sent me."

The demon laughed and snarled, "Your masters treat you like a puppet!"

Damien smiled, "At least my master's don't bind me and keep me from having free will. I can refuse them."

At that, the demon flipped the table onto Damien and lurched forward to attack him. Damien kept hold of his cross and dived to the side, landing on the floor with the cross held out from him. The demon jumped at him, and the cross struck him in the chest, causing him to scream out in pain. The demon began to dissolve back into his own plane of existence, but not before he reached out and scratched Damien with his hellish claws. The claws ripped down Damien's arm, causing a deep gash, and blood began to pour from the wound. Damien fell backward in pain as the demon returned to a mist form and descended through the floor.

Damien laughed out loud and said, "That was easier than I thought it would be."

Damien collected his artifacts from the floor and placed them back in his satchel. As he put his things away, he noticed that the gash in his arm had stopped bleeding but instead had a thick black liquid running into the laceration and began to travel into his veins. He quickly tied a handkerchief around his upper arm and pulled it tight to stop the flow of the blood and the black liquid. Once the handkerchief was tied tightly, he banged on the door to be let out.

Damien yelled, "The demon was sent back to hell. You can open the door now, Vicar."

Vicar Thomas opened the door and said, "So it is all complete?"

Damien pushed past the Vicar and snapped, "Yes, have my payment sent to Vivian Ambrose."

As Damien quickly moved away, the Vicar called out but was not heard, "And the child?"

Damien did not hear what the Vicar said and continued on his way to the residence and apothecary of Vivian Ambrose, the local healer he could trust.

Chapter 2

Damien knew the injury he sustained could only be healed by unconventional means. Vivian Ambrose was a healer he knew and trusted with his special medical care. Besides being a healer, Vivian was one of Damien's few friends and the one person he could, or already had, fall in love with. She was the one person who he could count on to heal any of the wounds he sustained and understood the nature of most of the same demons. She also had a keen knowledge of the weapons, spells, and poisons that the demons possessed. Vivian was also one of the few people he knew that he could trust with his secrets and keep his confidence. There were very few Damien trusted, and Vivian was the most trusted of all the people he knew.

As Damien made his way down the dark and empty street, his vision became blurry, and his blood felt as if it was catching on fire. Each step he took became more agonizing than the last, and his legs began to fail him. The street started to swirl under his feet, and the cool night air began to feel as if he was back in the Arabian Desert, where the nights could freeze, and the days could cook a person alive. Even though it was past midnight and not yet dawn, a bright light began to rise towards him and blinded him. Damien fell to his knees, gripping his temples as the burning in his blood reached his head. This was the last thing he would remember before waking up with cool water running down the side of his head. Damien fell back to sleep just as soon as he awoke.

Damien slowly opened his eyes and in the dim light he was delighted to see the beautiful, familiar, auburn hair lady softly sponging the sweat from his body. He could see the profile of her face through her hair and knew those soft and seductive blue eyes were looking over the entirety of his thin and muscular body. As his vision began to clear up, his mouth was still dry, and he could feel the cool sponge running down his chest and onto his stomach. The beautiful lady tending to him moved the sponge across his stomach and stopped just below his navel.

Without turning her head, she smiled and said, "I see by your reaction that you are awake and feeling better now."

Damien gave a sinful smile and replied, "I was enjoying the sponge bath and did not want to interrupt you."

Vivian turned her head to his face and said, "You can do the rest yourself." She tossed the sponge at Damien's face with a giggle.

Damien laughed and said, "You're no fun today."

Vivian returned the smile and said, "Too bad you slept through the last three days." Then she stood up and walked away from the bed.

Damiens's mind began to race as he tried to comprehend the fact he had been asleep for three days. How did he get here? What was it that made him sleep so long? Was there anything he missed? These questions and more raced through his head, and the pain in his head increased with a throbbing. Damien put his hand to his head and rubbed his temples, and at that, the searing pain in his forearm traversed up to his bicep. This triggered the memory of the demon slashing his arm with its claw. Then, the vision of the demon disappearing back to its plain of existence filled his head. Damien knew he needed to write this down as soon as he could so as not to lose any information.

Damien looked across the room at Vivian and asked, "What was inside me that put me down for three days?"

Vivian simply replied, "Ebontoxin."

Damien looked at Vivian, very confused, and murmured, "You're telling me that Noctherion the Blackvein was here on our plain and attacked me?"

Vivian turned and slowly walked towards him with his clothes, saying, "Unless you know of another way to transfer Ebontoxin, then yes, I am."

Damien, even more confused, uttered, "Why would the inquisitor for the Sovereign of Shadows be here, and here without his protective guards to boot?"

Vivian looked at him and said, "I am guessing that is a rhetorical question," as she handed him his clothes.

Damien took his clothes from her and said, "Yes, it was. I need to get back home and do some research."

Damien stood and made his way to the door. Vivian said, "You may want to put those clothes on before you go out the door."

Damien looked down at his naked body and replied, "I guess that would be a good idea."

Vivian helped him with his shirt and said, "The Vicar sent over your payment, and it is too much for what you owe me. Let me get the rest for you before you go."

Damien gripped her hand, kissed it, and said, "Keep it for what is to come. If what I am thinking is going on, you will need to have a good stock of supplies."

Vivian blushed a bit and replied, "I hope for the both of us that the next time is not as serious as this time. I would love for us to have some time to enjoy each other again."

Damien took her in his arms, hugged her tightly, and said, "I feel the same, and maybe next time, there will be no need for medical attention." He gave Vivian a small kiss as he let loose of her and turned towards the door.

Vivian looked at him with hope in her eyes and said, "One day, maybe you will really mean that and come home to me."

Damien turned back to Vivian and gave her another kiss, this one a little longer with a little more emotion behind it. Damien held her hand for just a moment longer and gave it a squeeze before he opened the door and walked out into the night. He wanted to look back and see her one last time, but Damien knew there was much to figure out, not just their relationship. He closed the door behind him and made his way down the empty streets of London towards his home. He played the scenario in his mind of him and Vivian getting married, him coming home to her, and a child after teaching a class. He also knew that this was not possible because the two things he learned about Vivian were that he does love her, and the second was that he could not bear to lose her in childbirth as his mother and the other Blackwell wives had suffered this fate.

Damien continued down the street, his mind wandering back to his new situation. Why was Noctherion there, and where were his protectors? He knew or thought he knew that this demon never left the safety of his guard or his lair. If Noctherion had come to the material plain, it could only mean that the primary demon he served had him question someone he could not recover to bring back to the plains of Hell. If this was the case, then the person was either well protected by a holy person or that the person possessed power beyond that of the Sovereign of Shadows. If the latter was true, Damien needed this person on his side. Also, if a holy person in London was protecting someone, why was he not informed about it? Damien's mind began to create scenarios of him questioning the Archbishop of Canterbury, William Howley. With every thought, Damien could only speculate what plans are in the works within the seven layers of Hell.

Chapter 3

Damien arrived at his home, which had been passed down for generations, and was filled with volumes of books and some handwritten journals from each Demon Slayer before him. As soon as he entered the large two-level terraced house initially purchased by his Great-great Grandfather, Thomas Blackwell, in 1734 with money granted to him by the House of Hanover, King George II's royal family, he felt the weight of history. This home, The Blackwell Estate had been established in 1520 by Damien's 8th great-

grandfather on the outskirts of London, had burned, losing most of the information from the Blackwell family before the late 1600s. Thomas collected some of the journals and scrolls created by his ancestors, but hundreds of years of information were lost. In exchange for the money given to purchase this home, the land of the old Blackwell estate was given to a farming family to make room for more crops to fill the reserves for the people of London. It remains, to this day, an active farm.

He entered his doorwayand went past the entrance hallway outfitted with a hall tree for hanging coats and hats, a stand for umbrellas, and nothing more. The hall tree had several coats and hats for different occasions and types of weather. There was also quite a collection of umbrellas since Damien always got caught in the rain without one and purchased a new one for each bad storm that came. At the end of the hallway, he opened glass-inlaid French doors that made their way to the home's parlor. Since this was a bachelor's home, it was more of an office, library, and anything else that one did in their home. He often did not even make it to his bedroom to sleep, and the couch was also his bed. For the first time that he could remember, a smell in his home reminded him of the stagnant air in the underground tunnels and old meat. Perhaps it was time to find someone to clean for him, but he did not like it when others moved his things around. Nevertheless, he needed someone he could rely on to care for his home since he could not find the time to clean up after himself, but this would have to wait until he had time to call for a service.

With that thought out of his head, he made his way to the shelf of books containing the research he would need to find more on Noctherion the Blackvein. Damien knew where the Blackvein existed, his purpose, and who he served. He did not know if it was normal for him to venture out of his plane of existence to the material plain. Damien knew from his past reading that there was more information on the Blackvein, but he was not sure which book held the enigmas of his existence that he needed to unravel that mystery. His library consisted of several books on history, religion, the occult, and other oddities of this world and beyond. The bookshelf he was looking at consisted of journals, notebooks, books, and guides created by his family. Many of the books were ones his great-grandfather had written down all the information he could recall after the fire. There were also the works of his grandfather and his father.

Each generation of Demon Slayer would write down any information they learned about what they encountered and edit any information they could on past notes. Damien had been adding his information to his journal. After he wrote down all he could remember from an encounter, he would go back and look over the past information to see if there was already information that he could update, and if not, he would put it into his book of information. This was the family's way of ensuring the best of knowledge gets passed on to the next generation of Demon Slayers.

Damien began to look over the books on the shelves and recall which one contained the information he sought. A book titled "Demons of Hell," written by his great-grandfather, caught his attention. He pulled it off the shelf and flipped the pages. He had read this and recalled that there had been no edits he could remember. The information in this book was almost unchanged since the original creation date of 1760. This made him think that either the information was the most accurate of all the information collected or that no other Demon Slayer had encountered any of the demons it contained after his great-grandfather.

Damien continued to skim through the pages of a handwritten book until his eyes caught a drawing with the caption, "The Sovereign of Shadows." He had remembered that Noctherion the Blackvein served under the Sovereign. The passage on the next page gave a background-origin and description of the prime demon:

"The Sovereign of Shadows is a prime demon of unparalleled power and cunning. It is a being cloaked in enigma and feared in all realms and planes of existence. Sadly, the true name of this demon is lost in time, and since the true name is unknown, no name can be used against it. Using any of the names it is known by will not render the demon powerless against anyone as others when the name is used to control them. I call the demon "it" because no gender features of male or female exist to define the gender of this demon. This demon, The Sovereign of Shadows, is genderless, most vile, merciless, timeless, and pure evil."

Damien recalled the rest from memory from when he studied this as an apprentice Demon Slayer. This was one of the leading books he read when he needed to gather information for the questions his father and grandfather would ask him. He continued to flip through the pages of the manuscript but did not find any reference to the demon he just faced. After taking one last turn through the pages, he returned the book to the shelf and looked over the rest of the book titles to see if anything caught his attention. As he looked over the books, one book bound in red leather caught his attention, and he felt as if the book was calling to him. Damien was not as familiar with this book as the others, but it was titled "Subservient Demons." This is a book he also had never made any updates to and could barely remember even reading it.

His father started this book before Damien was born, and it looked like he was still working on it when he went missing. Damien began to flip through the pages, and he was not even skimming the pages as he had done in the other book, but he felt as if something was guiding him to a certain part of the book. As he flipped through pages and pages of information, he saw drawings of demons that he had faced and several he had never seen in real life. All the demons looked familiar to him from his studies, but it started to feel like he knew them all more than just in the pages but in real life. Damien came to a page with the Noctherion drawn on it, and his hand just stopped turning the pages as if it was deciding where to look and not his eyes or mind. Damien began to look over and read the page carefully.

It read, "Noctherion the Blackvein was once a feared demon and was close to attaining prime demon status by overthrowing the Sovereign of Shadows. With Noctherion's powerful mind control abilities, he lures the Sovereign to a pit in his plain of Hell, where the followers of Noctherion wait to destroy him. As the Sovereign arrived at the location it was beckoned to, all the lesser demons surrounded it, with Noctherion leading them and controlling them with his mind. The hoard closed in to tear the Sovereign of Shadows apart by his limbs and sever his head, the only way the Sovereign can be destroyed; it began to laugh and drew its blade, slicing easily through the hoard of lesser demons, then turning the point of the blade to Noctherion the Blackvein's neck. Defeated by the Sovereign, he was made to swear allegiance and serve as the Sovereign of Shadow's interrogator for eternity. Noctherion had no choice but to comply since he knew his mind control was useless on the Prime demon.

This only served to amplify the power that the Sovereign of Shadows commanded, making him even more feared and respected amongst all the plains of Hell. Having such a strong interrogator who could extract any secret or minuscule piece of information from any mind made the rule of the Prime demon unchallengeable. To ensure his allegiance, Noctherion cannot travel without a set of guards to protect and bind him to his servitude. The demons are the most physically strong of all the demons and have special helms that block Noctherion's psychic abilities."

Damien took a step back from the book and took some time to ponder what he had just read. The description brought more questions than it answered. The questions that he already had about what he had just faced were now making less sense than before. The question of why he was here on the physical plane grew to an even larger question, along with why his guards were not with him. Had he been sent here on a mission, or was he escaping on his own? Damien was now wondering why Noctherion did not just use his mind control on him and bend him to his will, or did he do something to his mind and allow himself to be sent back to Hell? He knew that if Noctherion had taken control of his mind, he could have easily defeated Damion. Something was missing, and the mystery just grew larger and more complex.

Damien continued searching for more information in all the books on the shelf, trying to reassure himself that he did not miss anything relevant to this situation. While he was reading and conducting his research, there came a knock at the door, and it was a knock that sounded very urgent. He marked his place in the book he was reading, stood up from the chair, and went to the door. While he was walking to the door, the knock came again, louder and more urgent than before. Damien thought it was a strange hour of the night for someone to come calling, but just then, he noticed sunlight coming from behind the curtains. Another sleepless night while researching and working on a case, something that he was no stranger to. Then again, he slept for three days, and there was much to catch up on.

Chapter 4

Damien pulled the door open, and a familiar young man stood outside holding a large envelope. The envelope had the crest of Kings College London on it, and Damien thought it was a few weeks early for the new class rosters to be available. Still, other semesters had filled up early now that his class had become a requirement for graduation in most degree tracks. Damien also thought that with the coming semester, more of his time would be consumed by giving lectures, reading over assignments, and grading papers. Even though teaching one class was time-consuming, it meant that he had access to research materials, grants, and a paycheck. Also, he was the one who proposed the subject matter to the college, and it gained the interest of the King, so not teaching was not an option that would be good for his future.

The young courier smiled, handed the envelope to Damien, and said, "Hello, professor!"

Damien smiled politely, "Hello, and thank you." He took the envelope in one hand and placed two shillings in the couriers with his other hand.

The young man excitedly said, "Thank you, sir!" Three pence was the most he had ever received for a tip until now, especially since he only earned ten shillings weekly from the college.

Damien returned the smile and said, "You are welcome." He nodded at him, closed the door, and turned back inside the house. It struck him as odd that the young courier was so excited to receive the usual two-pence tip he always gave him but thought nothing more of it.

He began to open the envelope as he walked back to his desk and realized this was more than just the roster for his next class. It also contained a letter from the college board regarding a raise in his wages, along with a letter with the wax seal of the college dean. His interest first went to the letter regarding his wage raise, which outlined that his weekly compensation would change to four pounds sterling. Damien thought this was a very high wage for a professor who taught one class. As he continued to read the letter, it gave no details but said the college dean would outline his new position for him.

Damien sat down at his desk and broke the seal on the letter. The letter was written in the dean's handwriting, which was unusual since his correspondence was done by dictation by his secretary and only signed by him. The letter was to the point and void of the usual pleasantries added by his secretary to make him sound more amiable than he was. It quickly pointed out that Damien's new position at the college would be the Department Chair of Religious Studies. The chair position of a new department at the college explains the significant pay increase. Also, the new department and course of study will begin this coming semester. The letter further outlined that Damien had until the semester to outline a new degree and all the requirements to maintain this position. The outline must include two major areas of concentration in religious studies and two minor areas.

Damien was tasked with developing a comprehensive course outline for each major, emphasizing a well-rounded education. The board of directors, including the King, will review this outline closely. The King's keen interest lies particularly in courses exploring the occult and the darker aspects of religion. Aware of the King's fascination with these subjects and their theological implications, Damien understands the need for careful consideration in crafting these classes. Recognizing the importance of inclusivity and balanced representation, Damien also acknowledged the necessity of incorporating teachings from diverse religious traditions. As the narrative of religious fervor unfolded, each faith contributes its unique perspective, revealing the enigmatic allure of occult secrets, the existence of lurking demons, and the profound intricacies of human spirituality.

Damien sat back in his worn leather desk chair, which held certain comforts from his father and grandfather. He considered the possibilities and the backlash he could receive from the position or not accepting his new situation. His mind began to fill with how if he did not take the position as chair, it could end his career as a professor, not that this was his only means of income, but it was the only steady means of pay and gave him certain benefits. Also, if he turned it down, the King could have a very negative opinion about him, which would affect his dealings with the Church of England. It seemed he was in no position to turn down the offer, which was, in all actuality, a decree from the King and board of the college. He knew that he only had one decision to make, and that was what the requirements for the new degree were.

Damien began to lay out the objectives and outline ideas for majors and classes to accompany them. As he was writing out his ideas, he picked up the roster for his next class and saw that only twelve of the thirty seats were filled. This brought a new anxiety to him for the creation of a major, and he would need help to make this a reality. As he read the names on the list, two were familiar to him. Beatrice Whitehorn, the daughter and apprentice of Elanor Whithorn, was a known witch who practiced positive light magic and was an acquaintance of his. The second name was Annie Wright of Dorchester. Annie was unfamiliar to him, but her family was familiar because he had once done work at their home, and they are an affluent family in the United Kingdom. Possibly, they could assist him in filling the other seats in the class and get the word out for the new major, along with ninety more seats to fill.

After writing down a few ideas and coming up with possibilities, he realized that he would need to focus on his upcoming class to make it as attractive as possible and bring a new life to his academics. He would need to be very creative in his lectures and the subject matter. The students coming to take this class could be the ones to fill the seats in the new classes or tell others what they are learning, especially if they know of someone who would be interested in the subject matter as a degree. He thought that there would be twelve students in this class, just as there are twelve jury members when you are on trial. This is precisely what the class will be for him: a trial of his ideas, knowledge, and the twelve jury members. They will decide the fate of his future employment as a professor.

Chapter 5

Damien began to think that combining his current research into the Blackvein, The Sovereign, and their possible intentions into a research project could make the class more exciting and provide new, clear-minded perspectives. He could combine the study of the three major religions and this case to make the case their final research project, even put them into research groups and add it as an extra class credit. Damien could get help with his research and build a new class all at the same time. As long as each student earned a research credit along with the class credits, it would still fall within the code of ethics for the college. To keep himself within the confines of his contract, he would need to offer the research credit in lieu of a final exam for the class. Now, he just needed to update his lectures and prepare them for the class in two weeks.

After he had worked on his lectures for a few hours, Damien wondered if Vivian would listen to them and give him some feedback. She was the closest thing to a colleague or peer that he had in this field. This subject matter would not be well received by most other professors at the college. Most of the professors at the college felt his subject matter should not even be taught. Damien had similar feelings towards many of their subject matter but felt most of the material was outdated and could be more useful if modernized. Several of the subjects that were required to complete certain degrees have no usefulness in the fields of study they are associated with. For instance, why does one need to study differential geometry to get a degree in literature? He assumed it was a way for the math department to fill its seats. He will not make classes like these requirements for his programs, but he is not the math chair married to the English chair.

Damien's stomach reminded him that it had been about four days since he had an actual meal. He got up from his desk and made his way to the kitchen. While looking for something to eat, he realized it had been about a week or so since he had visited the market. Damien found some eggs, bread, cheese, and dried meat. At least it was something he could make a substantial breakfast out of. As he began to prepare his food, the strange feeling of being watched fell over him. He figured hunger and fatigue could get the best of anyone, and he would rest after eating. After he had prepared his food and cleared the dishes, he splashed his face with some water since the shadows were now moving in the corner of his eyes. His belly was satisfied, and his mind was still weary.

He walked into his library, cleared books from the couch, and laid down to take a short rest. As soon as he was comfortable, Loki, his cat, jumped up on his chest and lay down purring. His neighbor always ensured that Loki was fed while Damien was away, but the cat always knew when Damien was home. Damien stroked the small black cat and scratched his ear. Loki had decided to live in Damien's house when he came through an open window one night about two years ago. Damien woke up with the cat curled beside him in his bed. That morning, Damien gave him food and water, then set him outside when he left for the day. He had assumed the cat would go back to his home, but for three nights and days, this pattern repeated itself. Damien had ensured all the windows and doors were closed, but the cat still found his way inside. Damien decided that the cat had decided he would stay with him. Damien decided that since Loki was the god of mischief and trickery, the name fit the small cat. Loki was now a part of the Blackwell family as much as any other that lived in the house.

Chapter 6

Loki stood on Damien's chest, stretched, and jumped to the floor. Damien woke up after what felt like several hours, but it was only two hours. This was more than enough to help him reenergize and get his mind back in sync with his body. It was also just a long enough nap for Loki to work up an appetite as he pawed at his bowl, reminding Damien it was empty. Damien stretched as he stood from the couch and returned to the kitchen to fill Loki's bowl. As Damien filled the bowl with bits of meat and other table scraps that he knew Loki loved, he gathered his thoughts about the classes and thought it would be an excellent time to make his way to his lecture hall and work there for a time. He was hoping this would give him some more inspiration.

Damien gathered up his papers and put them in his satchel, along with some biscuits wrapped in a napkin. He walked outside, locked the door behind him, and flagged down a hackney carriage to take him to the college. As he sat back in the carriage and told the driver his destination, Damien noticed Loki sitting on the outside ledge of a closed window. It seemed as if he would never figure out how Loki got in and out of the house, but it made him wonder if the cat was just a cat. The carriage ride to the college takes just under ten minutes, and in that time, Damien had come up with several things that the cat could be, including a spy for the Sovereign himself. This was not likely, and Damien knew he was letting his imagination run wild, but sometimes the mind needed an escape. At that time, the carriage arrived on campus near Damien's lecture hall building.

Damien stepped out of the carriage, paid the driver along with a sizable tip, and said, "Could you come back tonight at about eight o'clock or send someone to fetch me?"

The driver said, "My shift ends at nine, so I will be here to pick you up, sir. Thank you very much."

Damien said, "You're welcome. See you tonight."

The campus was empty at this time of the year but would soon be filled with students from all over. Next week, the first-year students will come to the campus for their introduction to the college and receive their housing. They will also get prepared for all their classes, and the student relations office will show them how to get around all the buildings on campus. Then, towards the end of the week, the rest of the students would return to the campus and prepare for the next semester. For now, it was just the staff on campus, and it was usually quite tranquil.

Damien entered his office and unloaded his satchel onto his desk. He began to review his class itinerary and make notes for the additions to the class. All the changes he was making would lead the instruction into further classes for the new degree program. The first thing Damien did was change the name of the class from *"A Study of World Religions"* to *"An Introduction to Religion Studies and The Occult."* This title would tie both areas of study into this class as an entire introductory class, and combine the interest and controversy into one exciting class. Also, since the occult was a word that the King and Catholic hierarchy used to get people's attention, it tied it to both indirectly.

Damien had decided that he would keep the top three religions as the focus of the class and add the introduction to the occult as a separate section. The class would continue to give a brief overview and introduction to each religion and the same for the occult beliefs of each religion. To do this, he will have to shorten each section of the three religions so that new information can be added, and the removed information can be added to create more advanced classes. This will help him build the new curriculum and give him an idea of who should teach these classes.

After a long day in his office and as eight PM approached, he had his syllabus decided, and the course curriculum cut into the section he felt necessary for the new introduction class. The new course introduction and syllabus read as follows:

Introduction to Religions and the Occult

37

This course explores the diverse religious beliefs and occult practices prevalent in current times of the most prevalent countries of the world. This class will delve into Catholicism, Judaism, Islam, and the occult movements. The outcome of the course will be that each student will have a basic understanding of the history, core doctrines, rituals, holidays, and impact on society. This is an introduction and not an advanced study of any area outlined, but more advanced classes in each area are offered for further study. This class is required for the degrees focusing on the Religious Studies, International Business, and Industrial Welfare tracks.

Course outline:
Week 1: Introduction to religion and occultism
Week 2 - 3: Catholicism
A.   Historic content
B.   Basic doctrine
C.   Key figures and theologians
D.   Influence on society
Week 4 -5: Judaism
A.   Historic content
B.   Basic doctrine
C.   Key figures and theologians
D.   Influence on society
Week 6 -7: Islam
A.   Historic content
B.   Basic doctrine
C.   Key figures and theologians
D.   Influence on society
Week 8 -9: Occultism
A.   Historic content
B.   Basic doctrine
C.   Key figures and theologians
D.   Influence on society
Week 10 -11: Reflections, presentations, and exams

With the introductory class reorganized, the syllabus created, and the content leaving an opening for more advanced classes, Damien collected his things and made his way out for the carriage waiting for him. He also knew that with this task accomplished, he could send a copy to the Dean, and while he waited for a response, he could continue his research into the current events. On his way out of the building, Damien dropped the envelope containing the course information and addressed it to the Dean in the campus courier box, which was to be delivered in the morning.

Chapter 7

On the other side of London, in Vivian's home, the fire from the lamps filled the room as the sun set. Vivian prepared a meal for her mother and her that she would share at her mother's bedside. Margaret Ambrose was eighty-six years old and had been bedridden for almost a year now. Vivian had been taking care of her mother long before she became bedridden. Amos Ambrose, Vivian's father, had passed away ten years ago along with her three brothers in service to the King. Her father died two days after her twelfth birthday in the War of Sixth Coalitions. Her brothers followed in their father's footsteps and served the crown, and all perished in different military engagements. The youngest of the three brothers was the only one to marry. He and his wife, Cynthia Leigh, had a son to carry on the family name. Jamos Ambrose was only two years old and lived with his mother in Edenbridge, Kent, where her parents owned property and helped care for them both.

Vivian was several years younger than her brothers, and she spent most of her time with their mother and learned about her trade. She is proud to carry on the tradition of healing as the sixth generation of lady healers on her mother's side of the family. She longs to have a daughter to pass the tradition on to but also knows that if Damien was her true love, she would be the last of the line. If she sets aside her feelings for him and finds another to marry, Vivian could pass on the lineage of her bloodline to a daughter, and several suitors are interested in being that man. Her heart was torn between having her true love by her side and continuing the Blackwell name or finding a husband she could be happy with to carry on her family traditions and grow old with.

With these thoughts in her mind, as they always are, she took the meal into her mother's room and set the bedside table for them to eat. This was the time of day when all thoughts went away, and she focused only on her time with her mother. Margaret and Vivian ate and relished memories from times past. The smile on her mother's face brought more joy to her than anything else in the world. They both know her death is nearing, and every moment was precious time between them. This time of day had always been her and her mother's favorite of all. It was just them, no customers, no work, and just joyful conversation with good food. After the meal was complete and they talked for a bit longer, Margaret grew tired and fell asleep for the night. Vivian kissed her mother and tucked her in, just as her mother did as a child.

Vivian cleared the dishes from dinner, quietly left the room, and returned to the kitchen. After cleaning all the dinner dishes, she returned to her work table to continue her study of the Ebertoxin that she had extracted from Damien. Vivian had two objectives for the study. One, she wanted to find a way to create an antidote to save those who are poisoned by it, and it is guaranteed a death sentence. Vivian also wanted to recreate it so she could manipulate the formulary and create a more powerful weapon to be used against the demons. Once recreated, she could easily add it to different forms of weaponry to be wielded against the demons, but it would need to be kept a very deep secret. She did not want the knowledge of the weapon to get out and be used against other humans. Keeping this a secret project will not only allow her to help in the fight against the demons but also ensure that she is the only one with the antitoxin.

One of the first things that Vivian noted about the Ebertoxin was that it did not react to heat, which would usually speed up the chemical reaction of a compound. Also, when cold was applied to it, the chemical compound slowed much more significantly than she had expected. She hypothesized that since the compound originated in the realms of hell, the average temperature of the material plane would cause a significant drop in temperature for the compound. So, in theory, if she were to bring a person's body temperature down below the basic room temperature, the spread of the Ebertoxin should slow significantly. Vivian would then need to figure out the chemical bonding agent in the Ebertoxin that made the blood cells die upon contact.

Chapter 8

In the depths of Hell, the Sovereign of Sorrows gathered his devoted demons and spoke more about his plans for the physical plane of existence and what he would expect from each of them. In a room of his dark and cavernous castle deep in the bowels of hell, surrounded by the flow of magma, the top demons of his following gathered. Amongst them are Zephyion the Shadowblade, Morgath the Dreadbringer, Anthrax the Undying, Azrzel the Infernal, Lilith the Bloodthirsty, and Kuloth the Malevolent. A gathering of the most feared, loyal, and respected demons in this realm. Each of these Arch demons brings a following of greater and lesser demons.

The Sovereign of Shadows entered the room and greeted his generals in the common tongue of demons, Netherese. "Welcome, my generals and my most trusted advisors."

Each greater demon responded in unison, "Greetings, my Lord."

The Sovereign began with, "My inquisitor has found a way for us to enter the physical realm in hordes instead of just one at a time."

Chapter 9

A few days had passed since Damien sent his plan to the dean, and he had now received the initial approval. The final approval would come from the Board of Directors, which the King oversaw, and he did not doubt that it would be approved. He began to make preparations in the lecture hall. The lecture hall consists of a lectern on a stage designed to boost the professor's voice so it fills the hall. In front of the stage and lectern were four rows of long desks with chairs for the students. Each row is lifted a little so that each student can see over the others. There was enough room for fifteen students, which makes this one of the smaller lecture halls in the school.

While Damien was putting things in order inside the lecture hall and writing notes on ideas that came to him, the door burst open. The Vicar, Rabbi, and Imam rushed into the lecture hall, looking for Damien. When the door burst open, he looked up from his desk and saw the men approaching him quickly. He could tell that they had something of great importance and urgency to talk to him about.

Before the men had stopped walking towards him, Damien said, "Hello, gentleman, to what do I owe such a grand visit?"

Imam Ib al-Nabi al-Siddiq responded with, "as-salamu alaikum, Mr. Blackwell."

Rabbi Saloman Menckelbaum said, "Shalom Damien."

Vicar Thomas said, "Hello, Damien. We need your help on a matter of great importance."

Damien set his pen aside and said, "Please give me the details, and I will see how I can assist all of you."

Before the three men decided to come to seek Damien, they had met to discuss what was going on in the communities. Along with the common issues of poverty and hunger, a new issue had arisen. Children began to go missing without a trace or any clues as to how they were taken or where they had gone. The Metropolitan Police Service and Sir Robert Peel could not find even a shred of evidence. Scotland Yard sent its best investigators out with no results. One investigator, Mr. Henry Smith, suggested to the Vicar that he contact the other religious leaders and get them all to speak with Damien. This information piqued Damien's interest, especially since someone from Scotland Yard was paying attention to what he dealt with. He was still unsure what his skill set could have to do with locating missing children, but he was sure that helping them was something he should do, no matter if it was supernatural or not.

The Vicar explained to Damien that the last demon he banished for him was holding a child in the house Damien was summoned to. That child was later found dead, and the medical examiner found his brain looked as if it had been consumed from the scratches inside the skull. The scratches looked like something with claws was inside his skull, but there was no evidence of an entry or exit point. There was also a black residue inside of him that was not a part of any human anatomy. Damien knew what this was as soon as he was told but decided not to say anything. Damien feared that if he began to explain what he knew, it would only cause a panic more than was already in progress.

The Rabbi explained to Damien that there were two children dead and another missing in his community. All three of the children were one year old. The two dead children had no marks or visible reason why they were dead. They were found in their bassinets, next to the parent's beds. Neither set of parents heard any noise in the middle of the night, nor did the children wake them up with any fuss. The missing child bassinet showed no evidence of disturbance. The only similarity between the three children was their age and the family's religious beliefs.

Damien said with a very intrigued look, "At first, I was unsure what help I could be for missing children, especially more than Scotland Yard. Perhaps there is something more in my expertise that could explain the disappearances or at least reveal a clue of a more insidious nature. Imam, what has happened in your community?"

The Imam nodded his head and began to explain the situation in his community. Damien listened intently to see what similarities he could pick out between the Imam's situation and the Rabbi's situation. In the Islamic community, one child had died in the same manner as the one in the Jewish community. However, none have disappeared from the Islamic community. As the Imam continued, he explained that there was a child that may be possessed. The child's family was an important part of the community for butchering halal meats and making olive oil. The father is the only halal butcher in London, and the mother is the only olive oil maker. The community relies on them for the foods that can be consumed by the Islamic people. Since the home is regularly blessed by the Imam, it was believed the demon that possessed the child was caught in the home.

Damien responded, "Let me gather my things, and I can meet you at their home tonight."

Imam al-Saddiiq looked at Damien and said, "I would like all of us to meet there tonight after

Maghrib, the evening prayer. Is that agreeable with everyone?"

They all agreed to meet at the family's home, and as the Imam departed, he said, "Ma'a as-salam"

Rabbi Menckelbaum nodded and said, "Shalom and see you tonight," as he exited the lecture hall.

Vicar Thomas followed the other men and said, "I have a blessing to do this evening and will be along directly after. Be blessed and see you tonight."

Once they had departed, Damien gathered his things and took a carriage home to prepare. This would be the first time he had dealt with such a young child being possessed, and he was very torn about whether to bring all of his weapons. He knew that his Islamic artifacts would be necessary but was concerned about the child's fragility due to the age and how much damage the possession had caused. The last thing that he wanted was to be blamed for the death of a child and live with the guilt that he could not save them. Damien would need to plan carefully and be as cautious as he could in this situation.

Once he arrived home and collected his things, Damien brought all his usual items just in case. He would explain that the sword was only used once the demon was out of the child and did not return to Hell upon being exercised. Damien also decided to consult Elanor before going tonight and ask Vivian if she would join him at the family's house. Having Vivian onsite may not only help the child medically but possibly ease the parents' minds a bit more. She had a comforting demeanor, and her calming energy seemed to flow among those she was with. Damien gathered all of his things and left immediately for Elanor's house.

Chapter 10

As Damien knocked at her door, Elanor was sitting down for a noontime meal. She had a fresh loaf of wheat bread and Red Leicester cheese. She paused and considered not answering the door, but something inside told her she needed to. Elanor sighed as she set her fresh cup of tea down and went to answer the door. She could see the silhouette of a man through the shade she had drawn down when she closed for her meal. She pulled the shade aside to see who was at her door, and when she saw it was Damien, she knew it was the right decision to answer the door. Elanor unlocked and pulled the door open.

Before Damien could say anything, Elanor said, "I have a pot of tea, fresh bread, and cheese on the table. Please join me and eat before you bring up any business."

Damien said, "Thank you. I appreciate the offer." He walked in, set his things down, and joined her at the table.

They shared a small meal while discussing London, the weather, and recent news. This was something that Damien was not very good at and did not enjoy. Elanor knew this and carried it on longer than she had intended to see him get a little more uncomfortable, a game she enjoyed playing with him when Damien interrupted her day at inconvenient times. Damien had little social cues and was very awkward in social situations since most of his time was engulfed in his work and skills. After Elanor felt she had put Damien through enough torture and could see he was almost uncomfortable enough to leave, she asked him what was the reason for his visit.

Damien explained the situation to Elanor and asked for her consultation on anything she thought could be relevant. She explained that this was not a situation she had ever encountered and could be the first of its kind. The only information she could give him was an old prophecy amongst the dark witches that foretold the return of the most powerful of all demons in this century. Still, this prophecy seemed too early in the century to occur. The moon was not in the correct phase, and the planets would not be in the proper alignment for at least a year. Elanor said she would consult other witches of her order and see if there was anything they could contribute.

Elanor got up from the table and went to one of her workbenches, where she began to grind and mix some plants. She placed a small silver necklace on the tabletop, whispered a few words that Damien did not understand, and rubbed the blended concoction on the necklace. The necklace glowed a dim blue for just a moment, and the silver seemed brighter now than most of the silver jewelry he had seen. She placed the necklace on Damien and told him it would help protect him from the darkness she felt but would only last until the next moon rose. Damien thanked her as he made his way out the door. He tucked the necklace under his shirt, knowing Elanor would only do this if she felt a powerful darkness coming. He began to make his way to Vivian's house.

Vivian was returning to work after a noontime meal with her mother. Damien walked through the door, and she greeted him like a customer without looking. He greeted her back with a very familiar sound in his voice. She knew that something troubling was going on and was scared to turn and see if he was injured again or if it could be something worse. Did he find another woman to be the one he comes home to every night, the one that lays next to him, or the one that will carry his child? All of this crossed her mind in a split second. She took a long, deep breath and turned to look at him. She saw no visible injuries, and her heart sank into her stomach.

Damien faked a smile and said, "Vivian, I need your help saving a child."

Vivian looked at him intently and said, "Let me get my medical bag ready."

Damien said, "I think we need to talk about the situation first, as it has many unknowns." He motioned her towards the chairs nearby.

Vivian said, "I will put on a kettle for tea and join you at the table."

Damien set his things down, sat, and waited for Vivian to join him. Vivian returned to the table after putting the kettle on to boil, and she set out a plate of jumbles.

Vivian said, "The jumbles are my mother's recipe and are not only a good sweet but also have energizing herbs mixed into them."

Damien said, "Thank you. How is your mother doing?"

Vivian replied, "She is doing as well as she can, thank you for asking."

Damien smiled and said, "Let me tell you about the situation that we are in now."

He began to tell them all that the religious leaders had told him and what Vivian had told him. In the middle of the explanation, Vivian retrieved the kettle and poured tea to go with the jumbles. She listened intently and gave input where she felt she had something to offer, which was not much since this was a new situation with many unknowns. With everything explained to her and the little bit of information he had to offer and nightfall just a few hours away now, he asked if she would accompany him to the family's house.

Damien said, "I feel you being there will be a comfort to the family, knowing a healer is close by for their child, and it could be a very dire and lethal situation for me."

Vivian replied, "Let me go next door and get Grace to take care of dinner for my mum and stay with her for the night."

Damien said, "I will cover any cost that you have."

As Vivian walked out the door, she looked over her shoulder, smiled, and said, "I know you will."

Damien said, "I don't know if I like that tone in her voice." He continued to drink his tea and eat the delicious jumbles.

After about thirty minutes, Vivian returned and said, "Grace, the teen girl next door, will come over and care for my mum. She is a lovely girl who enjoys reading to my mum. Her grandmother taught her to read and passed away just a year ago, so I think it makes her feel like her grandmother was still with her."

Damien said, "Sounds like a nice girl and very helpful."

Vivian replied, "She is very sweet. Having a daughter like her would be a dream."

Damien tried to act like he did not get the hint and said, "Maghrib starts at sunset and ends when the red has left the sky. That is when we are to meet at the family's house. I believe sunset is about three hours from now, so do you mind if I nap here before we go?"

Vivian said, "Make yourself comfortable and remove your boots so they are not on the furniture."

Damien said, "I will remove them, and you should also try to get a nap so you are not tired. We don't know how long this will take."

Vivian replied, "I still need to prepare, so if I have time, I will nap. But I will prepare some energizing tonics just in case."

Damien removed his boots, laid down on one of the beds used to care for patients, and drifted off to sleep. Vivian gathered things she thought would be good in her bag and made a few energizing tonics in case they were needed for the night. After putting everything together, she still had about two hours left, so she decided a short nap would be a good idea. She decided to lie beside Damien and put her head on his chest. Almost instinctively, Damien wrapped his arms around her and pulled her close. He was warm, and she knew under the clothing he had on was a muscular body that she had patched up several times. Vivian closed her eyes and could picture his bare chest and well-defined muscular build, which he kept in shape by working on his fighting skills. She felt this was how she would love to spend the rest of her nights. Wrapped in his arms and listening to him breathe and the rhythm of his heart beating as she drifted off to sleep.

Damien woke up just an hour after Vivian lay down with him. He saw her in his arms and stayed still, holding her close to him. He knew this was the life he wanted, but he also knew he could not lose her. Damien knew what his life was meant to be, and love was not in the plan for him. He wanted love and Vivian to be that love, but with the destiny of his family line, he could not risk her life. For now, he would enjoy the warmth of her body against his and dream of the life he wants. Those are thoughts for another day, and today, there are bigger concerns to take care of.

Vivian began to wake up, and Damien gave her a gentle kiss on the forehead and said, "Best nap I have had in a long time."

Vivian smiled, rubbed his cheek, and said, "Too bad we have important work to do."

They smiled at each other, slowly got up from bed, and gathered their things. They looked into each other's eyes, smiled, and walked out the door. They stood outside in the setting sun and began to walk towards the family's house that needed help. Nervously, Vivian reached and took Damien's hand in hers. He did not pull away but lightly gripped her hand.

Damien said, "Don't worry, I won't let anything happen to you."

Vivian replied, "I am not worried about me."

Chapter 11

As Vivian and Damien approached the house, he let go of her hand, and she knew it was because he did not want anyone to think there were emotional bonds that would hinder his work. The sun was almost entirely set, and the red in the sky was just a wafer-thin line. Maghrib was almost over, and they stood quietly looking at the community of people who had gathered outside the home to pray together. Neither believed in any one deity, but they understood faith and respected other's beliefs. They also knew the importance of the prayer in the situation Damien was about to undertake. He did not need to be a man of their faith but to have the trust of those he was there to help. Mutual respect was a large part of his family's success in being demon hunters.

Once Maghrib had completed, the Imam introduced Damien to those who did not know him, and many blessed him and Vivian. He introduced Vivian as a healer capable of healing supernatural wounds; she was the only one he trusted for his care. Vivian smiled when he said this to everyone, making her beam with joy inside. The people showed her where she could put her things and set up a make-shift trauma site for what may happen tonight. She set up with the help of some women who were nurses during the war as Damien spoke with the religious leaders and the family.

Damien walked over to Vivian and said, "When I go inside the house, I will need you to ensure everyone here follows my instructions. I cannot be interrupted in any way. That would make it more dangerous for me and everyone here."

Vivian said, "You have my word."

Damien smiled at her and said, "You are not just the most important person here to support me, but the most important person in my life."

Damien turned and approached the house with a very stoic demeanor. The Imam and the boy's father were standing near the door, ready to open it for him. He walked up to the men at the door, turned toward everyone there with a very calm and commanding voice, and said, "Vivian is the best healer I know. She has saved my life countless times. She will be the one to assure the health and safety of the child inside. She will also be in charge of things out here while I am inside. I must demand that everyone stay out of the house no matter what they hear, and this door is to be locked until I have completed the task at hand. Continue to pray your prayers, and do not lose hope for the boy's safe return."

The Imam looked at the parents and said, "If Damien can put his trust in her, then all of us can trust her also."

The Rabbi and Vicar walked in just at the moment with followers from their communities and spoke in agreement with the Imam. The people of each community began to mingle into one crowd, and it seemed any differences had faded away in that moment. The religious leaders of the communities stood proudly next to each other, looked out at the crowd, and smiled with the joy they felt. This was a rare and glorious day for everyone in all communities. The separation of religious beliefs was overcome for the good of the children and the safety of all families in London.

Damien walked around the house's perimeter to get a feel for what was outside, just in case the fight spilled out of the house. In the back of the house was a patio with an outdoor stove and a minaret on the shared space between the house and the mosque. This holy area could be a great place for a final stand. Damien would have more power here, and the demon would be disadvantaged. He hoped the fight would remain inside the house and keep the demon in the smallest area possible. Knowing the surroundings gave him more advantage since he believed the house's blessing would limit the demon's vision to just his physical surroundings.

Once he had completed his observation of the home's perimeter, Damien returned to where everyone was gathered. The crowd had grown in size since he walked around the house, which made him even happier knowing more prayer would be going on. Damien approached the boy's parents, where Vivian and the religious leaders were talking. Damien went over his instructions again with all of them to ensure they understood the importance of keeping the house closed up with him inside. Damien also asked the parents for information on the inside of the home. He needed to know if there were any hidden rooms, religious artifacts, or anything new that could have been a portal for the demon. The only thing they could think of was a small storage space dug under the butcher shop with an entrance in the center of the floor in the butcher shop.

With all this information in his mind, he turned to Vivian and said, "Once I enter the house, lock the door and only open it if you hear me speak the words I said to you the first time you saved my life."

Vivian looked at him with fear and confidence and said, "Words you have lived up to, and you can trust I will not let your work be interrupted."

With that, Damien squeezed her hand and walked inside the house. She closed the door behind him, locking it as he asked. An ominous chill filled the house along with the smell of fresh cut meat, fragrant spices, and just enough light to make out shapes of the objects in the room. The moon was almost full and glowed into the windows, but small candles were lit in the kitchen where he had entered. It was eerily still inside the house and silent, too silent as if something was suppressing sound. The only sound he had heard was the clicking of the lock then not even the sound of his own movement could be heard.

Damien began to move towards the child's room keeping his hand on the hilt of his sword just in case. Each step he took was methodical and cautious for he did not know what he may face. He made his way to the door of the child's room where there was a line of salt on the floor blocking anything unwanted from exiting or entering. Damien decided to remove his overcoat, hat, and bag here. This is where he would prepare himself to enter the room and face the demon inside the child. He could sense great evil beyond the door but he could not determine what type of evil may exist inside that room.

Chapter 12

As Damien prepared to enter the child's room, he could hear voices from inside the room. There were two distinct voices, but he could not distinguish what was being said, and it did not sound like any language he had ever heard. He paused just outside the door with his hand on the doorknob, listening to see if he could determine how many beings or people were in the room. Only two distinct voices were speaking in deep, guttural, crackling, and haunting voices. Their sound even made someone as attuned to the darkest of things as Damien shiver just a bit.

Damien continued to listen to the indecipherable conversation for anything he might pick up on. Only one word spoken was in a language he understood: his name. Along with his name is what he could only guess was an invitation inside the room. Now he knew that his presence was known and no element of surprise was his for advantage.

The voice from inside the room said, "Damien is just outside the door and must not have understood our invitation to enter the room. It seems the Demon Slayer does not understand our language. Why does he not enter and test his skill against ours."

Damien opened the door, stepped in, and said, "It seems you have me at a disadvantage. You know who I am, but I do not know who you are. How should I address you?"

The smell of feces, urine, and vomit bombards his senses. Damien sees a young child lying on the bed with ropes holding his hand and feet to the bed posts. There are long straps of blood and sweat-soaked cloth, like a sheet torn into strips, across his torso and tied underneath the bed. The other furniture in the room is tossed aside and broken like it was thrown with a lot of force. On the right side of the bed sits a bedside table with an Islamic statuette of the crescent moon and star atop it. Evidently, the demon that possessed the boy had been exercising its powers to attack items in the physical realm. They seemed unable to move the holy symbol, which was of great importance to Damien. This demonstrated that the symbol had been blessed and could be a catalyst for divine intervention. If the demon had been capable of destroying the holy symbol, it would show that it was a major demon he was dealing with.

Just after Damien stepped into the room, the temperature began rising as if someone had lit a fire under the floor. This part was familiar to Damien as it seemed to be the demon's first tactic to impart fear into people. Not only had it been from his experience but also from the writings and teachings of every Demon Slayer before him. "The Fire of Hell" was how it was referred to in all of the books and called a parlor trick that had never caused any harm to anyone. It was a psychological tactic used to weaken the mind and make a person more susceptible to possession.

Damien continued to make observations and mental notes of everything he had seen. He began to look over the child as he stepped closer to the bed. The smell was overwhelming, and there were fresh wounds all over his body. It looked as if the demon was trying to cut its way out from the inside of the boy. From the blood stains on his night clothes, Damien could surmise that the boy was sleeping, and the demon found his way to him in his dream state, which meant the boy was likely still living in the nightmare created by the demon. The weaker the mind and body get, the stronger the demon becomes, and it can eventually take the physical form of the child permanently.

The boy's mouth moved, and a dark voice came from within him: "You know us; we have met before, and still, your thoughts betray you, Damien."

Damien shook his head in disgust and said, "You're just a revenant. A slave to the Sovereign who is trying to redeem itself from whence I beat you before."

The boy's mouth echoed a dark laugh and bellowed, "More powerful than you will be able to handle, like when you were a boy and peed your pants!"

With that information, Damien's mind began to race through his memories, looking for the event the demon had spoken of. Suddenly, his memory of himself in a room with his father is of him confronting a demon. This was the first time Damien had seen a demon in real life. All he knew of demons before were drawings in the books he studied. The demon grabbed young Damien, shook him, tossed him across the room, and it scared him so much that he urinated in his pants. He hit his head so hard it almost knocked him unconscious. Damien replayed the memory and tried to hear the name his dad used when he was confronting the demon. If he had the name, Damien could use that power over it and weaken it.

A second demonic voice came from the child, saying, "Search your feeble mind, little Damien, but you and I have never met, and it is not possible for you to defeat us both."

Damien continued to replay the memory over in his mind, but this was a distraction. He pulled his Karan out, held it towards the boy, and said, "Too insignificant to face me alone, so the Sovereign sent you with a babysitter? Even if you could defeat me, you are still a failure alone, Lazif!"

At the sound of his voice coming from Damien's mouth, the demon screamed in agony. The child howled in pain, and three voices now came from him. One was the deep sound of Lazif, another was a demonic yell from the unknown demon, and the third was the child waking from his nightmare. This showed Damien that he was correct about the name and could take this demon out with his words and even the odds in his favor. This also meant that the child's mind was awake and working on regaining his consciousness. Damien took this opportunity to bow down and began to pray an Islamic prayer for guidance and protection for the child. He prays loud enough to be heard out the window of the house, and the Imam begins to repeat the same prayer. The community members took hold of the prayer and chanted it as loudly as possible. The other communities start to pray in their faith, strengthening the power of all the prayers.

With the sound of prayer coming through the window in different languages, Damien came to his feet, held forward the blessed Islamic holy symbol, and demanded that Lazif release his hold on the child. With the power of the prayers and Damien invoking Lazif's name, his hold began to weaken. The boy's body contorted in ways that were unnatural for any human, and the boy screamed in pain. Damien touched the holy symbol upon the boy's leg, which he could reach, and demanded the demon release the boy.

Damien yelled, "Lazif! You have no power over this child anymore! Release him in the name of Allah! The people praying for power invoke the strength of Allah for the child. Release the boy, Lazif!"

More screams of agony came from the boy's mouth, but they were not his own. The demon's deep and guttural cries came from the boy's mouth, and words in a language Damien did not understand spewed from his lips.

Damien presented the symbol again and yelled, "Atliq al-qabda an al-walad wa atrik jasadahu. (Release the hold on the boy and leave his body)."

One demon yelled, "Lan tahzemeny (You will not defeat me)!"

With that yell, the boy broke free of the restraints. His eyes widened, his ears began to bleed, and a dark cloud of black smoke came from his mouth. The dark, hollow sound of a demonic scream came from the boy, and his body lifted off of the bed. A strong, powerful, and invisible force began to push on Damien as he held tight onto the bed. The cloud started to form a familiar face that had scared him so badly as a child. It was Lizif being pushed from the boy's body and trying to gain a physical form. The community members could hear the screams and began to pray louder and faster; some sang songs, and others held up their religious symbols. All of this combined gave strength to Damien and the boy.

Without warning, the phantasmal demon form of Lazif shot forward towards Damien. The demon's rage overtook his entirety, and Damien swung his blessed sword, striking the demon right through his head. As the holy blade passed through the gaseous mass, a bright blue light shone from the blade, and Lazif screamed in pain. The demon was banished back to Hell, and the boy's body fell limp onto the bed. Damien relaxed his grip and stepped forward to look at the child. He could not tell if he was breathing or not.

A feeling of dread came over Damien, and he lurched forward to take the boy's pulse. He could feel a weak heartbeat and see his chest rise just a little. He thought, "Could this be the defeat of both demons, or was he fooling me, and it was just one using different voices."

As soon as he turned to get help for the boy, his eyes shot open entirely black, and the boy grabbed Damien's arm. Damien screamed in pain from being squeezed so hard, and he could feel the bone crush. The boy shot up and threw Damien into a wall. He slid down the wall, hitting the ground hard. The boy laughed in that demonic voice and stood next to the bed. Just as fast as he stood, the boy fell to the ground, and a demon stood in his place. The demon stood six feet tall with dark red scalded skin like a dragon. His eyes were dark as night, with a red glow around them. It had horns that protruded up from its forehead and back above the head. Its teeth were elongated, sharp, and yellow. Its fingers were long with pointed claws at the tips, and its feet were hooves like a bull. This demon was not familiar to Damien.

Damien got to his feet, sword in his hand, and took an offensive stance, ready for the next move. The demon ran forward at Damien and swung his claws at him. Damien countered with his sword, knocking the blow away from him, but the sword made no mark on the demon's scales. It swung repeatedly, each time Damien parried the moves with his sword. It stepped forward, and Damien moved to the side, then behind, kicking the knee of the demon and slashing its neck with his sword. Its knee buckled under it, but the sword still made no mark on the scales. The sharp edge was useless against the scales of the demon.

The demon swung around, grabbed Damien by the throat, and lifted him from the ground. Damien struggled to break free of his grip, but the more he struggled, the tighter it became. He tried to stab the demon with his sword, but it was useless. Damien began to feel himself blacking out and, with all that he had left in him, ran his sword up and into the armpit of the demon. Finding a weak spot in the scales, the demon screamed in agony and dropped Damien to the ground. He struggled to catch his breath as the demon stumbled back, grabbing himself in sheer pain. Damien heard the demon mumble something and tried to listen closer.

The demon said, "Iblis, father, give me strength."

When Damien heard this, his mind raced, and he drew his small dagger blessed by the Vicar. He did not know if it would work, but he jumped on top of the demon and stabbed at the skin in its armpit. The demon grabbed at Damien's arm and they struggled for the dagger. Suddenly, a memory came to Damien, one from long ago that he had read in his great-great grandfather's book.

He pushed as hard as he could and yelled, "Thabor! Go back to your father!"

Thabor screamed in agony as the blade went up through his skin and pierced out his shoulder. He lurched his head forward and bit Damien in the chest. His teeth pierced deeply into his flesh, ripping and tearing at the muscles. The dagger began to glow a bright white light, and the smell of burning flesh engulfed their senses. Damien screamed in pain and, in an instant, began to blackout.

As he began to fade, Damien said, "Bi qudrat Allah ana atrodaka min hadha al-'alam." Then he fell on top of Thabor, son of Iblis.

About the Author

Lee Alexander, originally from Louisville, Kentucky (Seneca High School class of '90 IYKYK), and now residing in Virginia Beach, Virginia, with his wife and four children. He is a military veteran and an Information Technology professional. Lee is also an experienced Dungeon Master with over 30 years of experience in Dungeons & Dragons, which helped hone his love for storytelling. He holds a Master's degree in Information Systems and is pursuing a Doctorate in Information Technology. He has a passion for dark fantasy and gothic horror, which comes to life in his debut novella, "Shadows of the Past: The Damien Blackwell Chronicles." When not writing, working, or studying, Lee enjoys delving into historical research and ancient myths.